Animen Kingdom Books

1

The
Chronicles
of Tempo

Written by
J. A. Medina

Illustrated by
Suresh Maru

Contents

Copyright

One kingdom, One species, One Choice

The Chronicles of Tempo

Written by
J. A. Medina
Line illustrations by
Suresh Maru

Visit our website at
www.thechroniclesoftempo.com
First e-book and print on demand edition 2022

To Josh

Dear Josh, inside every one of us, live an Angel, a Human and an Animal, the Angel is kind, brave and strong, he knows how to separate right from wrong, the human, is intelligent and capable of achieving anything he set his mind to, but he is often afraid to do so, On the other hand, the Animal is wild, strong, and fearless. The question is, who do you want to be? the angel, the human, or the animal? The choice is yours.

Introduction

Once upon a time, somewhere far beyond the stars, there was a beautiful, magical kingdom named Tempo. It was inhabited by the two species of angels: the celestial angels and the angels of fire. At first, everyone lived in peace and harmony because there were a lot of rules and guidelines to follow.

One day, the angels of fire decided that it was time to create a new world, a world without rules, a place where people could do whatever they wanted, good or bad, without having to face the consequences. However, their decision led to a devastating war between the two species.

During the war, many angels lost their lives, and many more were injured. One day, as hundreds of celestial angels and angels of fire avalanched toward each other on the battle-field, the ruling god, angry for the fact that the celestial angels were losing battle after battle, descended from above, landing right between the two armies and shouted, "Stop!"

The impact of his celestial staff and the magnitude of his deep voice produced a massive wave that sent warriors flying in all directions. It also caused the ground to crack, separating the entire kingdom into two.

The celestial angels named their side Tempo, while the angels of fire called theirs the Kingdom of Fire. Worrying about the future of Tempo and the wellbeing of the celestial angels, the gods decided that it was time to breed a new species of warriors.

A creature strong enough to be able to fight the gods' hardest battles.

Not long after, the gods selected a group of their most skilled angel warriors and sent them on a mission to earth. The plan was to take back as many life form samples as they could find. After some time, walking among mankind, the celestial angels returned to Tempo, bringing with them humans, animals, plants, water, and soil. Straight after their return, the gods began to work on what they called the experiment. The purpose of the experiment was to merge the D.N.A. of humans, angels, and animals to breed the new species. Then, after seven days and seven nights, the new species was born, and the gods called them animen.

The animen looked like humans but were much taller and stronger. They thought like humans and even spoke like humans. The only difference was that the new species possessed the intelligence and magical powers of the angels, with the strength, ferocity, and survival skills of the animal, a D.N.A. so complex that the code could never be broken.

The animen were gifted with the power of transformation, the power of choice, and the power of magic, meaning that they could transform into anything without limitations if they made use of the powers of choice and believed in magic. However, the new species were only given a short life to live. The problem was that no one ever told them that they possessed such amazing powers.

Soon, the news about the creation of such a unique breed spread across the two worlds, attracting the attention of the angels of fire who immediately declared war over Tempo.

To protect the animen from their greatest enemies, those with the strongest percentage of human D.N.A. were sent to earth to live among mankind. Their mission was to use their superior intelligence and unlimited potential to help humanity and create a better world until the time was right for them to return to Tempo.

On the other hand, the animen with the strongest percentage of angel D.N.A were kept alongside the celestial angels so they could develop their combat skills. Only the ones with the most powerful combination of animal and human D.N.A. were relocated to the first ever animen kingdom, a place where they could grow and reproduce freely until the time was right for them to become the first generation of animen warriors.

As their lives were controlled by time, this new kingdom was named the Seventh Kingdom of Tempo, which translates to the Seventh Kingdom of Time.

The seventh kingdom was a place like no other. The water, the plants, and the soil taken from the earth recreated the look and feel of the human world, while fairies, dragons, and mystical creatures were brought into the land to give it a magical touch. After its creation, the kingdom was divided into four territories. These were the Triangle of Spectra, Tempo, also known as the forest of dead, Tundra, the forbidden land, and Vida, the invisible island – exactly where our chronicles begin.

Chapter 1
Initiation Day

It was a special day for the residents of Vida, the invisible island. Everyone seemed happy and uplifted. Peoples, fairies, and domesticated mystical creatures were on their way to the Fountain of Life. It was Initiation Day, the time when the younger generation of animen underwent a ceremonial ritual in which they and their families found out for the first-time which animal lives inside of them. The ceremony always took place right at the centre of the Fountain of Life with a huge crowd of spectators watching.

During the ceremony, the chanting man, who was one of the older members of the community, used a spiritual ritual to unleash from inside each of the youngsters the animal that would then become their animal centre. During the ceremony, the young animen transformed into the chosen creature for a short period before turning back into their usual human-like form.

At the village not far from the fountain, Angel was lying in bed. Suddenly his mother entered the room.
"Angel, Angel!" she shouted while extending her arms to wake him up.
"What now, Mum?"
"Do you know what day it is?"
"Yes, Mum, I know, it is Initiation Day."
"That is right, so get yourself out of bed now, we don't want to be late for that."

A few minutes later, Angel, his mum, and his pet, a ferret

named Ferret, joined the crowd of animen and creatures that were walking along the path on their way to the Fountain of Life.

"Mum, do you know which animal I will transform into?"

"Son, no one knows which animal lives inside of us until it shows up. However, today is the day when girls and boys will experience transformation for the first time. Look at you: tall, muscular, long arms, strong legs. You may well transform into a bear just like your father always wanted you to be." As she said that a look of sadness appeared on her face.

"Mum, why are you looking so sad? It is about Dad, right?" Faith kept quiet for a moment. "Was he indeed a great warrior?" "Angel, your dad was a great warrior, but he was also a great partner and a wonderful dad. Come here, I want to show you something."

After walking for a short period, they arrived at the edge of a cliff from where they had a clear view of the forest that lay far beyond. "Look down there, that is the island of Tempo, our home. Many years ago, after the creation of the animal species, the angels of fire declared war over Heaven. During that time, we saw thunder, lightning, and explosions, then huge balls of fire landed on the seventh kingdom, burning everything in their path. When the war ended, a wolf pack showed up in Tempo.

At first, they looked like ordinary wolves, so we ignored them, but then we discovered that they were searching for the medallion of Tempo."

"What is the medallion of Tempo, Mum?"

"Son, the legend said that the medallion of Tempo is a great sort of magic. It possesses the secrets of the seven days and seven nights. Whoever possesses the medallion has unlimited access to the power of transformation, the power of the choice and the power of magic."

"Is that why the wolves want it so much?"

"I don't know, son. What I do know is that Wolves were afraid of magic, however, they already possessed the power of transformation, so they had a great similarity to us. Look at the Fountain of Life," she commanded. "For us, to transform from our animen form into animals, we must chant and give thanks to the gods. Only then do we get to experience the powers of the transformation. However, the wolves could transform from animals into monsters in a matter of seconds. They also had a strong alliance with another deadly species the bats. They too were searching for the medallion."

Angel's mum continued. "I still remember it as if it had happened yesterday. When the wolves and bats began attacking Tempo, there was nothing that could stand in their way." At that point, she recalled the monsters storming through the forest, the screaming, the fire, and the atrocities that she and her people witnessed during that time. "Our warriors, including your father, fought with all they could to protect our people."
"What happened then?" asked Angel as his face illuminated with anticipation.
"Luckily for us, Vida, the angel of life, opened the magical bridge that connects Tempo with the invisible island, allowing us to cross into this side of the seventh kingdom. However, not many of us managed to make it into this side of the kingdom."

"Does that mean that there are still people out there?"
"Yes, there are, and the sad thing is that for some of them, time is running out."

Chapter 2
Chosen

Bald Kea the eagle girl was hunting on the proximities of Tundra, the forbidden island, when she spotted an injured creature on the other side of the river. Somehow, she knew how dangerous the forbidden land of Tundra was, but she was not afraid of anything.

After flying to a tree nearby, Kea took another look at the creature. The youngster looked like a wolf but was not a wolf; his skin texture was very different, his head was big, his claws were large and curvy, and the shape of his tail was also very estranged. It looked like a cross between a bear, a wolf, and a dragon. What in Heaven is that thing? she wondered. At first, she wanted to ignore it and carry-on hunting, but she knew that the young, injured predator had no chance of surviving on his own, so she could not re-sist the temptation. Having made her decision, she looked around trying to locate any member of his species, but there was no one around. At that point, she wondered how the youngster reached that end of the forest and how long he had been there for. The answer was a mystery like the millions of mysteries hidden in the forbidden land of Tundra.

Kea would normally carry prey much bigger than her, so the young animal was not a problem. At that point, she dived in the direction of the young creature. Then, using her skills and her powerful talons, the eagle girl grabbed the youngster. As she lifted him, she decided that it was going to be dangerous to just land on the other side of the river, so she flew back to the Orphanage of Tarragon.

After leaving the creature in a safe place, she walked to the training camp where her friend, Kormo, usually trained to develop his combat skills. He had amazing abilities and incredible senses. His reactions were improving day by day; his body was strong from head to toe. From a young age he had mastered the art of the staff. He could climb trees, jump off cliffs, and run through the forest without injuring himself, but what made him extra special was the fact that he was blind.

"Kormo, I have something to show you," she shouted. For a couple of minutes, the boy kept jumping around, knocking things down, and cutting in the object that his trainer was throwing at him from many different angles. When the training came to an end, he turned his attention to her. "Kea... what brought you here today?"
"I have something that I want you to see. Come on, we don't have all day."

As they started to walk, Kea began talking to him. "Hey, don't you wish that one day, you could transform into that fierce panther that lives inside of you?"
"Yes, I do, but we all know that it will never happen unless we find the power of transformation," he replied.
"Do you think so? What if we already possess the power inside of us?"
"I don't know," he replied. "What I do know, is that our time in this world is running out."
"What about you, do you wish you could transform into a real eagle?" Kormo asked.
"Well, sometimes, but to be honest, I am happy the way I am."

As they got closer to a location nearby, Kea then told him all about the injured animal. This time the excited boy almost forgot his condition. I want to see it, he said. On arrival, the boy placed his hand on top of the young creature. Immediately he had a vision of what the animal looked like. He is beautiful; I have never seen something like it. After a short inspection, the boy helped Kea to take the young animal inside the orphanage for treatment. When they got inside, he prepared a mixer of herbs to treat the young predator's external injuries.

"What is going to happen to him now?" Kormo asked.
"I need to take him back to Tundra," Kea replied.
"You can't do that; he is very fragile. If you take him back, he is going to die out there."
"Kormo, you may be right, but we can't keep him here," Kea said.
"I said we keep him until he gets a bit stronger, then we can let him go. There is nothing wrong with looking up to a dog."
"Yes, I know, but this is not a dog, look at him. He looks like a beast. Who knows what this thing is going to turn into when he recovers? Trust me this thing is gigantic. By keeping him, we may be putting everyone in danger."
"But, Kea, we are already in danger. In fact, danger is all we know. Please let me keep him, please?"
"Ok, you can keep him, but as soon as he fully recovers, you must send him back to the wild, do you understand?" Kea said.
"Yes, I do understand. As soon as he gets stronger, I will let him go," Kormo agreed.

Back on Vida, the invisible island, the animen were singing and chanting to the gods of Tempo. "Hi lala, hi lala, ole ole mo, hi lala, hi lala, ole ole mo! Gods of Tempo, gods of Tempo. Thank you for the power of transformation." The chanting was complemented by a group of animen with red and green colourful paint spread over their faces, playing on drums and unusual musical instruments.

During the ceremony the chant called the youngsters one by one into the fountain to conduct the ritual. The first one into the fountain was a girl. At first, she was a bit nervous, then, as the transformation started to take place, she became agitated. Her hands started to open, giving way for her animal centre. Suddenly from inside of her came out a roar. At that instant, she transformed into a lioness. The noise and the excitement of the spectators was incredible. After her, it was time for a boy to walk into the fountain. During the day, many youngsters transformed into, lions, horses, birds, and many other animals. "Come closer, boy," said the chant man to Angel when his time came. As Angel got inside the fountain, the sky started to turn dark, then the ground started to shake as if something terrible was about to take place. At that moment, Angel could feel something possessing his body as if the transformation was occurring from the outside and not the other way around. His hands were turning big, something wasn't right, his body temperature started to increase. He felt hotter than ever. As the crowd kept chanting, Angel could no longer hear anything.

At that point, Angel started to feel a hypnotic state taking over his body. His mind and soul were transcending to a parallel universe, a place where he had never been before. He was going beyond his animal transformation and converting into something else. The old animen stared at the rushing water of the fountain for a short period. "The current shouldn't be like this," they murmured, "there is something odd about the way it is flowing."

While the confusion intensified, the spectators kept
chanting and dancing with curiosity: "Hi lala hi Lala hole
ole mo, hi lala hi Lala hole ole mo. Gods of Tempo, gods of
Tempo, thank you for the power of transformation." At the
same time, the sky kept closing in, causing more thunder
and lightning. Somehow the lightning was forming a
fireworks-type atmosphere. Different colours and light were
flashing above the fountain, and suddenly lightning struck
the fountain directly.

"It could only mean one thing–" said the chanting man,
but before he could finish his sentence, a powerful force
dragged the boy to the deep waters. Looking from the side
of the fountain, Angel's mother was desperate to see her son
coming back up from the deep. Suddenly there was total
silence as the boy came back to the surface.

At that point no one said anything, but it was clear that everyone was surprised. Angel appeared to be bigger, more muscular, and stronger. His leg was built like the soldiers of the supreme battalion that once upon a time defeated the army of supernatural snakes.

He was supposed to transform into an animal. Instead, he transcended into a bigger and stronger being, but that was not all. The boy emerged from the deep waters wearing the medallion of Tempo. "What is going on, he is supposed to transform into an animal!" shouted some of the spectators. However, for the chant man, something was clear: the boy was without a doubt the chosen one.
"The prophecy was right," he said. "Among the animal species lives the one who will save us all."

Shortly after Angel emerged from the water, the chant man walked to him. "Angel, the gods have chosen you to carry the medallion. You must travel to Tempo immediately, find the rest of our people, and reveal to them the power of the transformation. Farewell, young Angel, all our hopes go with you." As soon as the chant man finished his speech, more thunder and lightning struck, then the magic bridge of Vida opened like a rainbow. Suddenly a magic circle formed around the boy.
At that point, Angel turned his attention to his pet. "Ferret, I will miss you my boy, please take care of my mother while I am gone." Then he spoke to his mother. "Mother, I will do everything in my power to save our people."

"God bless you my son, I know that you will make us proud." After the final goodbye, Angel's body vanished in a spectacular tornado of energy, leaving no trace of him. No one knew in what direction the magical bridge had taken him, but everyone knew that it was time for the young Angel to make his journey into the unknown, at the mercy of the medallion of Tempo.

Chapter 3
The arrival

A few days had passed since Kea let Kormo keep the young predator, so she went back to check if he had indeed let the animal go back to the forest. When she arrived, he was finishing his shift at the orphanage where he worked, helping to look after the young orphans . As soon as she arrived, the kids became excited. "Kea, Kea," shouted some of the kids, while everyone rushed toward her.

"Nice to see you kids," she said while struggling to keep her bow and quiver away from them.

"Welcome back, my dear friend. I thought you had forgotten us, what brought you here today?" asked Kormo.

"I came to check on you," Kea replied.

"I am alright, thanks," Kormo said.

"What about the young predator, did you let him go back to the forest?"

"Well, I tried, but he kept coming back, so I let him stay with me. He has turned out to be such a good boy. I called him Sarchus."

"That was not what we agreed. I am not happy about that, but to be honest I am glad you kept him. The two of you shall make a great team, and I am looking forward to seeing him again."

"All right, let's go then," replied Kormo with a bit of excitement.

A few minutes later the two friends arrived at the Temple of Tarragon. "Here we are, home sweet home," Kormo said.
 After walking through some of the corridors of the temple, they arrived at a back area where the animal was kept

tied up with a chain around his neck. "Hey, boy! Look who is here, our friend Kea." The animal stood still for a few seconds, then after a short inspection, he remembered her. Immediately he walked toward her with excitement, then started to lick her face with his massive tongue while moving his tail from side to side.

"Oh my, you are gigantic. Kormo, this thing is bigger than us. Looking at him I do think that the two of you will make a great team, but don't think you are ready to hunt yet, because you are not."

"What do you mean? You have seen me at the training camp, I am ready."

"No, you are not. At the training camp, you guys are training to become warriors. To be a hunter you need different skills," Kea informed Kormo.

"Come on, how hard can hunting be?" Kormo asked.

"Kormo, hunting is harder than you may think. Anyway, speaking of hunting, I am going into the woods today."

"Where exactly are you going?" Kormo asked.

"I am going somewhere dangerous."

"Where, tell me?"

"Are you sure you want to know?"

"Yes, please."

"Well, I am going deep into the Forest of the Dead."

"What, are you serious?"

"Yep, it has been a while since I went hunting on that end of Tempo. I have a feeling that today will be a good day for me out there."

"What about the wolves, are you not worried about them?"

"Me, worry about the wolves? No way."

At that moment, Sarchus got agitated. "Easy boy, easy," said Kormo. "Do you see, he gets agitated when he hears that word. Do you know that by going there you are putting yourself in danger?"

"Yes, I know, that is exactly why I am going there."

"Alright, fine, but please promise me that you will be careful."

"Ok, I promise. Anyway, I shall get going now, it is getting late. Say hello to your dad for me."

After the conversation, the two friends walked out of the temple. Shortly after, they arrived at a particular spot, then they embraced in a long hug. "Beautiful as always," he said. "And you? As charming as usual," replied Kea before taking into the sky in the direction of the Forest of the Dead.

Sometime later, Kea arrived at her destination. At first, she flew around in circles while scanning the ground with her eagle eyes. After a few minutes, she flew down into a tree, then she spotted a wolf pack. "Here we are, creatures of the night, she said to herself. You and I alone in the Forest of the Dead."

Moments later, the wolves started to walk toward an open plain, as they needed to go across into the next part of the forest. As the pack took to the plain, Kea noticed that they were carrying a wooden cage. At the point, she descended at a tremendous speed while shooting at her target, then she landed on the ground. At that very moment, two very aggressive-looking wolves ran toward her. When they got closer, she took four arrows out of her quiver. She waited for the right moment, then shot them all at once. As the arrows struck their bodies, the massive wolves started to howl in pain. Then, she shot again and again, until the creatures were down.

After Seeing that, the rest of the pack started to transform from monsters into four-legged wolves, then suddenly, they decided to run away, leaving a wooden cage behind.

Moments later, after taking a lot of precautions, the eagle girl looked inside the tiny cage. Inside there was a fairy. She forced open the cage to free the magical creature.

"Thank you for saving my life, young lady," said the fairy.

"My pleasure," replied Kea, while inspecting the bodies.

"Do you have a name?" she asked.

"My name is Crafty; I am a male fairy."

"Crafty, why were they taking you?"

"Wolves kill fairies because they are afraid of the power of magic," said the male fairy. "Somehow, they think that by exterminating us, magic will be wiped out from the animen kingdom, but that is impossible. Do you know that our dust can be used as a powerful sort of magic?"

"Not really, but if you say so, I believe you. In fact, I could do with some magic myself."

"Well, speaking about magic, you have proven to have a good heart, so Crafty wants to bless you with a gift."

"Like what?" Kea asked curiously.

"Close your eyes please," said Crafty. As Kea closed her eyes, Crafty sprinkled dust all over her quiver, and began talking in a strange language.

"Hey, what are you doing?" Kea asked.

"Crafty has dropped some pixie dust inside your quiver, so from now on, you shall never run out of arrows. And one more thing, every time you hit a creature, big or small, it will turn into stone. Oh, Crafty almost forgot. Your arrows are now under your command. Whatever you ask, they will do. They could even follow their target for miles and miles until they reach them. However, those arrows will never put down an innocent creature, not even by accident."

In another part of the forest, Angel had landed at an unknown location. The problem was, he could not remember his name, where he came from, or what was he supposed to do in this place. The smell of fresh water, the sound of the birds, the spookiness of the forest, and the mystery of his surroundings all indicated that he was in a dangerous location. Something that got his attention was the fact that the wildlife creatures, were desperate to get away from there. What is this place? he wondered. I must find my way out of here as fast as possible. As he started walking, he could feel the presence of someone or something moving around the trees. Everything indicated that he was being watched.

A few minutes into his walk, a rustling sound caught his attention. As he looked up to the trees, Angel could not help but feel a wave of panic; it was the first time he had found himself alone in the forest. As he kept moving forward, the bushes seemed to be reaching out to grab him. "What is happening to me? Why do I keep seeing things? My head is playing with me."

Moments later, he heard a strange noise from above. "Who is there?" he shouted as he looked around, trying to find out from where the sound was coming from. This time his heart filled with dread. That place didn't feel right, and he was sure that something awful was about to happen. Suddenly, two strange looking creatures landed right ahead of him, while a third one looked with a contemplating expression from a tree branch.

Their faces looked like rats but with long ears. Instead of arms they had long wings, but not like a normal bird. Theirs were sticking out from the side of their body like arms. The creatures had long skinny legs and short tails, their teeth were indicating a threat and their huge wings had paws sticking out of their shoulders with long nasty claws ready to kill.

Chapter 4
The chase

"Look what we have just found, wandering on the wrong side of the forest," said one of the creatures.
"Brother, what do you mean on the wrong side of the forest? This is the right side of the forest; it is our side of the forest." "Shut up, idiot, I am speaking in metaphor. What I mean is, what shall we do to him?"
"We are killers, right?"
"That is right, brother, we are killers. So, let's kill him."
At that point, the third creature descended from the tree. "Hey, we are not going to kill this one. Instead, we are taking him back to the cave, I have the impression that he is someone important. Not often does our prey fall from the sky."

"I am not afraid of you," cried Angel.
"Did you hear that, brother?"
"Yes, I did, do you think I am blind? Get him, idiot!" At that very moment, the creatures started to transform into something stronger, taller, and surely more deadly. After the transformation was completed, one of the creatures launched an attack on Angel, determined to catch him. Suddenly, it began to rain heavily. As the tension grew, another creature grabbed him and tied him with his massive wings. After some struggling, Angel managed to set himself free, then ran deep into the forest. The furious creatures started to chase him while making terrifying sounds as they shot arrows at him. One minute, they were running on the ground, and the next they were flying and running from tree to tree.

"Where are you, stranger? Show yourself, do not be afraid of us, we are good creatures."

"Why are you lying to him? We are very nasty creatures, aren't we brother?"

"Shut up, idiot. We are trying to confuse him."

"Oh, all right, yes, we are very good creatures. We do not kill animen, we slaughter them."

"Hey, your brother is always ruining the hunt. I do not want him hunting with us again."

"Oh, are we hunting?"

"No, we are playing hide and seek, idiot."

"Call me idiot once again and I will tell Mum and Dad when we get back to the cave!"

As their argument went on, Angel found an opportunity to run again. However, unfortunately for him, two more creatures joined in the hunt. They were faster and stronger than the other three, so soon Angel found himself tied up with a rope, leaving him no room to move.

After tying him up, the creatures started speaking to one another in a very strange language. "Motacota filmed halehaopen! Tutocoto Sligo." After inspecting him, the creatures prepared to take off. Suddenly, from somewhere above the trees, someone started shooting arrows.

"We are under attack!" shouted one of the creatures, wildly looking around, trying to identify where the arrows were coming from.

Suddenly, one of the creatures spotted Kea running from tree to tree as she shot arrows at them all. At this instant, the first creature was hit by an arrow. The creature broke the arrow and kept moving toward her, then just before reaching her, his body turned to stone. Kea then looked up as another creature approached from above before shooting him.

Immediately, his body turned to stone. Kea then jumped to the side, narrowly avoiding the massive rock falling over her. Soon after, four of the creatures were turned to stone, except one who managed to escape. "Follow him," commanded the shooter to the flying arrow. After the incident, there was a moment of silence.

Angel looked around. A young-looking girl landed in front of him.

She was tall with a strong body composition. Her white hair was short and messy, and she was carrying a nasty-looking bow in her hand and a quiver of arrows on her back.

"Who are you? And what are you doing in this part of the forest," Kea asked.

"I don't know. I can't even remember my name," said Angel. "Tell me the truth or I will kill you right here. Come on now!" she shouted with an aggressive expression while holding her bow with an arrow pointing in his direction.

"I am telling you the truth, I am lost and confused, I need help." Suddenly, Kea spotted the medallion of Tempo on Angel's neck.

"Oh my, I know who you are." At that point, without a word, the girl untied him. "My name is Bald Kea, but everybody calls me Kea. Come with me, I shall take you to a safe place."

"What species are you?" asked Angel.

"Don't you see? I am an eagle."

"What about the creatures, what were they?"

"They were bats, you are very lucky to be alive. Come on, we must leave this place immediately. We are not safe here, follow me."

Meanwhile, somewhere deep inside the forest, the wolves were hanging out in their underground cave when a bat arrived, as he landed on the ground, his body transformed into a human-like creature. "Master, master!"

"What is the problem?" said Marmaton the alpha as he approached the creature.

"He is here, I saw him with my own eyes."

"What are you talking about?"

"The chosen one, master, we saw him falling from the sky. He was wearing the medallion of Tempo."

"Impossible, why didn't you bring him to me?"

"We were going to, master, but we came under attack. The eagle girl was there, all the others got killed."

"So, you are saying that you ran away?"

"No, master, I just wanted to bring you the good news."

"You are useless!" shouted Marmaton. "Get out of my face." As the creature turned around to leave, the arrow that was following him struck on his chest, turning him into stone. At that moment the alpha let go of a very loud howl as his body transformed into a massive monster-like wolf, then turned his attention to the rest of his pack. He started to speak in his ancient language.

"Galloper whatmetoclia, semturoniam pe all coletedile scheme, femtilengo te brother site sister, le she Plato, f oretelling taletulaptero stronger, what site we pe wolves, bats we demafuloy, a mist to many but a legend to none, if worship exist, quiet our montemate we hot be watenfury force. Ting God turned Moira to bigolatin when put dim denied plus le power ou choice, change the contemner ou magic, sie also on life, put million ru tempo pe do only beans Pele bor, defense value so make puy fe lo time, she arrives now, tu brother le sister, catenary ou night, be Marmaton superman re out there ta casino le Medallion of Tempo."

Translated into English, this said: "Listen to me, creatures of Tempo, until this day the eagle girl had been hunting our brothers and sisters as she pleases. For generations our species has been strong. We are wolves and bats; therefore, we are monsters. We may be a mist to many, and a legend that no one thought could ever exist. We were denied the power of choice and the power of magic, but we possess the power of transformation. So, brothers and sisters, creatures of the night. I, Marmaton, command you to go out there and

ɔring me the medallion of Tempo."
At that moment some of the wolves started to transform into monsters. At the same time, the bats that were hanging head down on the roof of the massive cave and sitting high up on the rocks began to jump into the air. They too transformed into monsters before leaving the cave, making terrifying sounds in reaffirmation that they were also hungry for blood.

At the same time, on the other side of the forest, Kea and Angel had reached eagle land in the small village where she lived. When they arrived at the main entrance of the village, two adult eagles landed in front of them. They were very tall with a strong build. Their clothes indicated that they were the gatekeepers, on their hands, they had arrows and bows.
'Kea, what are you doing? We do not allow strangers into eagle land," said one of the keepers.
'I know that, but he needs help. This is the only safe place where he can spend the night," replied Kea.
'Who is this boy?" asked one of the eagles.
'He is the chosen one," said Kea.
'In that case, come in," replied the second gatekeeper.
Inside the village, Kea took Angel to a nearby tent. It was one of the only few built on the ground. "You will sleep here tonight. I shall come back in the morning to check on you."
That night was a bit difficult for Angel, and he struggled to sleep as he kept trying to remember who he was.

Chapter 5
Eagle Land

The next morning, when he woke up, he walked outside of the small tent. At first, he could not see any sign of life in the village. Everything was empty. Then, as he walked a couple of metres away, he was surprised to see the elders and the females watching him from above, stood and sat on the tree branches, while a child ran between the branches trying to get a glance of the stranger. Many of them had not seen an outsider for a very long time.

The village was beautiful. There were many houses constructed on the treetops.
"Kea, where are you?" Angel shouted while looking around.
"I am here," she said. As Angel looked, Kea was also sitting on a branch. "Come on up!"
"Who, me? I don't climb trees."
"Why not?"
"I don't know, I guess I prefer to stay on the ground."
"Come on, climbing is easy."
After trying for a bit Angel finally made it up to the tree branch. "I have to tell you, this place looks amazing," he said.
"Yes, I know, it is my home."
"Talking about home, can I ask you a question?" asked Angel. "Yes, go on."
"What do you eagles do? I mean how do you survive out here?" "Well, we are a fishing community, and a great percentage of our diet depends on fish. So, we spend a lot of time around the rivers."
"How do you do it?"

"Do what?"

"How do you eagle fish?"

"Why do you want to know that?"

"I don't know, I guess it is just curiosity."

"Adult eagles with the most superior ability and experience take Charge of the fishing. They fly to the rivers where they swoop down over the water and snatch the fish out with their talons. We have a special structure on our toes called speckles. It allows us to grab and carry prey that are sometimes even double our body weight."

"That sounds very interesting, but if you are a fish eater, what were you doing in the middle of the forest?"

"Who, me?"

"Yes, you."

"Well, I was hunting."

"Hunting for what?"

"I don't know, any creature that looks like a monster, I guess."

After a short conversation and a proper look at the village from their tree branch, the two of them returned down to the ground. "Come with me, I have someone I want you to meet," Kea said.

As they walked on the path, Angel asked another question. "Hey, why is everything so quiet around here?"

"Because the village is on high alert. We are on the lookout every hour of the day from the trees and the sky." She finished the sentence by pointing to various trees above which Angel could now see eagle warriors flying. As soon as the conversation finished, the two of them stopped at the main part of the village.

"Here we are, this is where our leader will meet you, come on in," Kea said.

When they walked inside, the leader was already waiting for them.

"At last," said the leader. "Boy, what is your name?"

"I don't remember my name sir. I don't know why this is happening to me."

The eagle man moved closer to him, then looked at the medallion on his neck. Then he turned around to speak to Kea. "If he is the chosen one, he shall make it alive to the Temple of Tarragon. It is the only place where he can find all the answers."

"But, sir, I thought that he could stay with us until he figures out who he is."

"Young Kea, only the gods know the answers to that question. What I do know is that the wolves may already be hunting him down. They are not going to stop until he is found. By allowing him to stay, we are putting our people in danger, so let his destiny speak for himself."

"Boy, you must travel to the Temple of Tarragon, take this map. It shall help you find the location of the temple. There is no time to lose, you must leave immediately." At first, Angel was concerned about crossing the Forest of the Dead, especially after what happened there the day before. Then he looked at the map. As he looked, tiny twisting paths sprung up like veins on the pale parchment. The green spots indicated the right path; the red ones indicated the dead zone.

"Kea, take him to the south of the forest. From there, he must make his journey alone." The leader turned to Angel. "You must go now."

"Come on, let's go, it is a long journey. We must make it to the open grassland before is too late," Kea said. "The wolves usually hunt at noon, so we must stay ahead of them."

Chapter 6
Ferret

Kea and Angel had been walking in the direction of the forest of tarragon. During the journey she kept teasing him by flying along the trees on the path, then walking from branch to branch, something that her companion could not do. When they reached a particular part of the forest, Kea stopped. "My friend, this path shall take you to the mountain of Tarragon. My mission ends here."

"Thank you," Angel said as a huge sense of panic ran down his throat.

"Just remember, if you see a creature that looks like a wolf, run for your life. Good luck, young warrior, we shall see each other again." At that instant, the eagle girl took off into the air on her way back to eagle land.

By the middle of the afternoon, Angel had reached the southern edge of the mountain. He was exhausted so he decided to take another look at his location on the map. As he did so, he noticed something that made him panic. There were massive footprints shown on the map that indicated that the wolves had been around that part of the forest, probably a few minutes before him. Suddenly, he heard a very loud howl. He took another look at the map. This time he could see the footprints coming toward him, and the green part of the map turned red. Then, just as he was about to get going into the opposite direction, he had the impression that something was following him.

As he turned around, a huge black wolf was standing right in his path, looking at him with a frightened expression. His ears were pointing forward, indicating a tread. Suddenly the wolf moved forward toward him. "Easy boy, easy," said Angel, as he stepped back trying to gain some distance from the animal. Moments later an opportunist launched his attack from behind, causing Angel to roll down a hill from the impact. Angel could feel the creature's sharp claws scraping his skin. Then, to prevent the creature from using his massive teeth, Angel held its huge head away from his body while using his leg to kick the creature. At that point there were wolves everywhere. Luckily, as his energy started to fade away Angel began to hear a chant resonating in his head. *Hi lala hi Lala ole ole mo, hi lala hi lala ole ole mo.* Where have I heard that chant before? Angel wondered.

As the chant became more and more clear to him, he started to remember: first the Fountain of Life, then Initiation Day, then his beloved mother. Only at that point did he finally remember who he was. "Angel, that is my name," he said out loud, before he started chanting. *"Hi lala hi Lala ole ole ole mo, hi lala hi Lala ole mo.* Gods of Tempo, gods of Tempo, thank you for the power of transformation." Angel was getting stronger by the second. It was clear that some sort of transformation was taking place, but what was it? Whatever creature he was transforming into, was strong.

After finding his strength, Angel managed to get up, then miraculously a supernatural force possessed his body. Understanding that the boy had become stronger, the wolves began transforming from ordinary looking wolves into monsters. As the creatures finally stood up on two legs, Angel was able to produce a massive magical wave with his bare hand that sent the wolves flying. As more wolves approached, he produced a circle of fire around himself for protection.

At that point, the wolves scampered around the circle trying to get closer to him, but there was nothing they could do. Noticing that the monsters were afraid of the fire, Angel started to walk toward them, burning everything in his path. Suddenly the pack decided to stand back. "Retreat, he is using magic!" one of them said. As the pack turned away, their bodies started to transform back into their normal animal form.

"We will be back!" shouted another of the creatures before vanishing into the forest. Moments later, Angel walked closer to the fire, then he extended his hands toward it, and instantly the fire stopped.

At that moment, Angel looked at his hands. He could not believe what was happening. "How come I can't transform into an animal, but instead I am able to produce fire? From where is all this magic coming from?" At that point, there were a lot of questions to be answered. After the encounter Angel decided to keep on moving. Suddenly, a tiny blue light appeared floating close to the ground. Then a magical door formed from the light. It was a portal. A moment later the floating doors opened, and a small looking animal walked out of it.

"Well done, my boy, Angel has made the first step to figuring out who he is." As Angel turned around, he noticed that it was his beloved Ferret.

"Ferret, how did you get here?"

"Young Angel, Ferret can travel through the passages of the parallel dimensions, a portal with no limitations. Ferret is here because Ferret follows orders from someone very special, someone who loves Angel unconditionally. However, it appears to Ferret that Angel is having trouble remembering who he is, and why he is here. Come with me, Ferret shall show Angel what Angel needs to see."

Two minutes into their walk, as they passed by what appeared to be a normal tree, they could hear some whispers.

"Did you hear that?" asked Ferret.

"Yes, I did. What is it?"

"The forest is speaking to us, the whisper is coming from that tree," Ferret said. As they got to the trees the whisper became louder, then Ferret placed his tiny hand on the tree. Suddenly a magical window opened, and he asked Angel to look inside.

"I have never come across something like this, what is going on?" Angel asked.

"Young Angel, this is the past and future memory of our world revealing itself to you. Look."

As Angel looked inside, Ferret asked, "What can Angel see?"

"I see a huge battle between angels and animen, massive creatures are landing from the sky, everything is on fire," Angel said.

"What else can Angel see?"

"I see images of myself as a child, the location, the clothes that I am wearing, the creatures around me. Everything looks so different from what I know."

"Okay, get your head out now," commanded Ferret.

"Wait, I see a man entering the room. He wants to take me away, but his body is on fire." At that instant, confusion and panic took control of Angel's emotions, so he took his head out of the tree.

"Don't panic, young Angel. What you saw there was the light and the darkness unfolding right in front of your very own eyes. Angel can't change the past, but Angel has the power to change the future. All Angel needs to do is to trust his powers, and his powers will trust Angel. Just seek the light and the light shall find you. Remember, inside every one of us there is an angel, a human, and an animal. The question is who do you want to be?"

"Ferret, what about the fire? How come I can be so comfortable with it?"

"Young Angel, unfortunately Ferret can't say any more. Ferret must go now." As Ferret said that he walked a few steps then started to look for something. "Oh, I found it!" he said. Suddenly, the blue light appeared, and it started to transform into the floating portal. When the magical door was fully formed, Ferret walked into the other side. Then, as he closed the door, the portal vanished.

Chapter 7
The Intruder

Angel was still a bit confused, but he knew that he needed to stay strong to fulfil his destiny. So, he stayed focused and commanded his powers to show him the way. He was amused when he noticed that the trees, which at first had been closing in on him, were now getting out of his way. It was a question of trust, and he knew that by trusting his powers everything was going to be alright.

By late afternoon, Angel had reached the southern edge of the grassy plains of the mountain of Tarragon. As he took another look at the map, he noticed that he was right there. "This is it. The temple should be here, but where is it?" Suddenly, he focused his attention on a massive rock ahead of him. Curious, he walked toward it, then placed his hand on it. Surprisingly, the rock started to move until a massive door opened on the ground. Angel was sure that it was the right place, so he began to walk down the dusty staircase.

On the way down there were spider webs everywhere around the walls. It was a sign that no one had walked down that entrance for a very long time. At that point he started to walk in the direction of the light that was coming from the other side. As he got closer to the main part of the place, he noticed that he was inside a massive cave. Then, as he progressed forward it started to look like a proper building. There were a lot of candles lit up and a lot of paintings on the walls showing different animen with arrows and bows, as well a few angels and Monsters statues all over the place, as Angel took a look up, there were also many beautiful paintings on the high roof. "This is great, I've never seen something like it," Angel said.

Suddenly some of the candles went off, then the shadow of an enormous wolf-like figure appeared in front of him.

As Angel looked on, the walls behind him closed, trapping him inside the salon. Angel produced a magnificent blue light in the palm of his hand to light the room up. As he stood still, he could see the shadows changing directions from one side to another. For a moment, Angel thought that he had walked into the wolf stronghold. However, there was no way back. Moments later the sound of a heavy chain made his body shiver with anticipation. It was clear that Angel had entered the creature's territory and was about to pay with his life.

Angry and ready to kill, the creature launched himself toward Angel. At that point Angel extended his right arm toward the creature. As he did, he produced a magnetic barrier between them, preventing the attacker from getting any closer. Luckily for him the heavy chain also prevented the creature from reaching him.

Angel was in a panic while the massive animal roared like a beast as it was trying to break free from the chain. Suddenly, from the other side of the temple, an animen approached. "Easy boy!" shouted the arrival. Immediately the creature came down. "Who are you?" asked the arrival.

"My name is Angel."

"What are you doing here?"

"I come from Vida, the mystical island. I am looking for the Temple of Tarragon."

"Come closer," commanded the arrival, as he held a strange-looking staff in his hands. He placed his hand on Angel's shoulder. Suddenly a flash-forward allowed him to see how Angel looked and showed him the medallion. "You are the chosen one. At that point Angel understood that the animen was blind.

"What is your name?" asked Angel this time.

"My name is Kormo, and he is Sarchus, my pet."

"How do you know that I am the chosen one?" Angel asked.

"I can't see you, but I sense the sound of your heart," Kormo replied. "Come with me, I shall introduce you to the others." Without hesitation, Angel followed him along the long corridors. For his amusement, there were a lot of animen inside the temple. As the two of them passed by, some of the animen kept looking at Angel like if they had never seen another animen before. Minutes later the two of them walked into a room.

"My dad is very ill, but he will want to hear everything that you have to say."

"Dad, there is somebody I would like you to meet."

"Come closer, boy," said the animen, turning his attention in the direction of the boys. "Boy, what is your name?"

"My name is Angel, sir." At that point, the animen, who, until then was laid in bed, tried to sit up.

"It can't be possible. What is your mother's name, boy?"

"My mother's name is Faith."

At that point, the animen started to cry.

"Father, what is the matter?" asked Kormo as he could hear his father crying.

"How is she?" the animen went on.

"She is fine, sir, beautiful as always, but why do you ask? Do you know my mother?"

"Angel, my name is Evenko. I am your father."

"Father, you are alive." At this instant Angel rushed toward the bed, then the two of them embraced in a long hug, full of happiness, mixed emotions, and a lot of tears.

"Could somebody explain to me what is happening?"

"Kormo, one year before we rescued you from the fire that claimed the life of your parents, I lost the two people that I loved the most: my wife, Faith, and my son, Angel. The son I thought I would never see again. Today, I thank the gods for bringing him back to me."

Angel then explained the reason why he had travelled to Tempo.

After the encounter Evenko took a moment to just hold Angel's hand. Then, he turned his attention to Kormo. "Son, first thing in the morning, you must take Angel to the deer village. When you get there, tell them that I need all the animen leaders here at the temple as soon as possible. Then, go to the gorilla kingdom and tell Mono to send his people to spread the word around, they will know what to do next."

Chapter 8
The magic Sword

The next day, the boys got up early then made their way to
the mountain. As they started walking away from the
temple, Angel had a question. "Hey, Kormo, how are we
going to find the deer village?"
"What do you mean?" he replied.
"I mean, if you can't see the way, and I am new around here,
how are we going to make it?"
"Don't worry about it, my eyes can't see, but all my senses
are wide open. We shall make it without a problem." After
some time, walking through the secret locations and hidden
paths, Kormo stopped. "Angel, did you hear that"?
"I can't hear a thing, what happened?"
"Something is wrong," replied Kormo. At that point Angel
looked around for a few seconds but could not see or hear
anything unusual, so they kept going. Minutes later, as they
reached the top the hill, they encountered something that
they would never forget.
"Kormo, you were right. The village is almost destroyed,
there is smoke coming out of the burned houses." Said Angels as he contemplated the villa from above.

As they walked around trying to find anyone who was still
alive, Kormo placed his hand on a tree. Instantly he had a
glance of what had happened there. Then, he heard a noise
coming from the bushes. When they went to the spot, they
found a young deer on the ground. His body had been
dismembered, but the animen was still alive. Kormo kneeled
to the ground, placing his hand on the deer's forehead
immediately he recalled what had happened to him. Seconds

later, the animen took his last breath.

"What happened here?" asked Angel.

"They have been attacked by wolves, some of them managed to run away to the top of the mountain. The rest have been killed or taken as prisoners."

The two of them were now walking toward the centre of the village trying to search for any survivors.

"When do you think this happened?" asked Angel while looking at the atrocity of the scene.

"They were ambushed not too long ago, they were not expecting it," said Kormo as he touched the ground. Immediately he visualised the number of footprints let by the wolves. "The pack may still nearby, come this way."

After tracking down the pack, the boys were in for a shock. At the centre of an open plain, the wolves were scampering around in narrow circles. Some of them had already transformed into monsters, while the others were still in their animal form. In the middle, there was a young wolf about to be burned alive.

"What is happening?" asked Kormo as he heard the fire and smelled the burning branches.

"They are trying to kill one of their own," replied Angel.

"It is not a surprise for me. Wolves have no mercy." At that point, Kormo stepped out into the open.

"Hey, we have got company," said the leader of the pack. The rest of the pack turned their attention to Kormo. The wolves were big and scary, but Kormo was not afraid of them. "Attack!" shouted the leader. Fearless and determined to get the job done, Kormo stood still as the creatures approached. He held on to his staff firmly, focusing all his senses to identify where they were coming from. A moment later, putting all his training to the test, he launched himself at the approaching wolves, without hesitation.

At the same time, Angel teleported in the direction of the fire to free the young wolf from it. At first, he was a bit surprised as he had no idea that he could teleport, then he remembered to trust his powers. He extended one of his arms and commanded the fire to stop. At that moment the leader of the pack started howling loudly, and in a matter of minutes some wolves showed up.

When the young wolf was free, Angel teleported again, but this time to free the deer who were still tied up. Moments later, the deer people joined the fight, but it was not sufficient. After some life and death confrontation, Angel created a magnificent blue magical barrier all around them, stopping the wolves from penetrating. At that point, the sky turned dark, then lightning and thunder began to strike. "Go back," shouted the leader of the pack, "they are producing magic. Let's get out of here." At that moment the remaining wolves transformed back into ordinary wolves before vanishing into the forest.

When everything was over, the young wolf started talking to Angel. "Thank you for saving my life."
"No worries," replied Angel. "What is your name?" he went

on. "My name is Dangerous," was the reply.

"Dangerous, why were they going to kill you?"

"They were trying to kill me because I refuse to kill innocent creatures. Just because I happen to be a wolf, it does not mean that I must act like them. Something inside of me tells me that I am not a monster."

At that point, Angel walked closer to the young wolf then placed his hand on his shoulder and said, "Young animen, inside every one of us lives an angel, a human, and a monster. It is up to us to choose which one to be. Your actions are right, however, if the pack finds you again, they will kill you, so what are you going to do now?"

"I shall go away to the forest of Moomba, just on the other side of the volcano. I will start a new life there, but I owe my life to you, so if you ever need my help, just call my name and I will be there for you." After his final words, the young wolf transformed back into an ordinary wolf before taking off into the forest.

Then, Kormo turned his attention to the deer. "My friends, go back to your village, try to save whatever you can, then find the others and let them know that my father wants to meet all the leaders at the Temple of Tarragon as soon as possible."

47

Chapter 9
Lisa the Glider

As the boys approached the part of the river from where they needed to make a U-turn to the gorilla kingdom, Kormo realised that they had been followed. "Wait, we have been followed. Quick, come this way." Using the advantage of the low light and his knowledge of the forest, the boys accelerated their steps, and they reached a small clearing from where they had to cross into the other side of Tempo. About twenty strong wolves approached from various directions. For the boys, there was no place to hide.

"So, here you are, chosen one, what are you going to do now?" said one of the wolves. "Consider yourselves to be dead," he went on.

Based on the number of wolves and the level of aggression that they were showing, Angel knew that his only option would be a weapon, so he wished that at that very moment he had a weapon. Suddenly, to his surprise, a magnificent silver sword appeared in his hand. Confused but glad, he clutched it tight as he looked up to the sky and gave thanks to the gods.

Surprisingly the wolves did not seem to notice the blade of the sword because it was invisible to anyone with dark intentions; all they could see was the handle. Immediately, Kormo came closer to Angel, then, holding his staff tied, he placed one hand on Angel's shoulder. That way he could have a glance of their surroundings.

"There are a lot of them, but no worries, we can do this." The wolves were closing in, so Kormo stood still as he held his staff tight. Then, as the wolves approached, he managed o locate their distance, location, and speed. A moment later, when the creatures were in a close-range, Kormo stepped to the side manipulating his staff with elegance, causing serious damage to the attackers. Understanding that the boys were stronger than they first thought, the hunters started to transform into monsters. Soon, more wolves joined in. At that point, the situation was proving to be too much for the boys. A few minutes into the fight, Angel and Kormo were standing back-to-back, preventing the monsters from getting any closer. Suddenly, somebody started to shoot darts from above. In a short period, a few of the wolves were killed by the shooter. The question was, who was it?

"What is happening?" asked Kormo, as he could hear the wolves as they were shot.

"Someone is helping us," said Angel. Moments later Angel could see an unfamiliar figure gliding from tree to tree while shooting darts. At that point he extended his hand into the ground. When he lifted it, magnetic waves sent some of the wolves flying. Then he ran toward a particular tree and said, "Tree of the forest, with the powers of the medallion of Tempo and the blessing of the gods, I command that you come alive." For a few moments nothing happened, then suddenly the tree branches started to smash the wolves like massive wooden hammers.

"They are using magic!" shouted one of the monsters as they kept moving forward. Then, from a place not too far away, another wolf howled very loud.

"We have to go!" shouted the leader of the hunters. The creatures started to transform back into four-legged wolves before running away.

When the fight was over, the magical sword vanished from Angel's hands. Intrigued about all his magical abilities, but tired and with some bruises on his body, Angel asked the stranger to show himself. "Show yourself, we mean no harm." A moment later from a tree a strange-looking creature came to the light. As the creature came closer Angel noticed that it was a lizard girl.

She looked young and skinny with dreadlock-like hair, her skin tone was bluish mixed with green and brown.
"Who are you?" asked Angel.
"I am Lisa, Lisa the Glider."

'Lisa, where do you come from?"

"I am from the Blue Kingdom!" she replied while inspecting the dead bodies.

"So, it is true that the Blue Kingdom exists?" asked Kormo this time

"Well, I think so. Did I say blue or green?"

"Blue, you said blue. So, yes, it exists."

"Wait, let me see you." Kormo said. At that moment he moved closer to her, then found her arm and held it tight. At that instant, he could see her face. "You are very young. What are you doing here alone?"

"I ran away from home," she said.

"Why?" asked Angel.

"Because I like to be independent, do you have a problem with that?"

"What about your parents?" asked Kormo.

"Parents, who needs parents? Those creatures are annoying, I am allergic to them."

"Anyway, do you guys ever get tired of asking questions? Are you going to tell me your names?"

"I am Angel, and this is my brother, Kormo."

"So what species are you guys?"

"We are animen," replied Kormo."

"I know that, but how comes I saw you using magic?"

"It is a long story," replied Angel.

"By the way, guys, how did I do? It takes serious skills to do that you know," Lisa asked.

"Thank you, Lisa, you did very well." said Angel. Your help came at the right time.

"Oh, thank God for that. I have been following you guys for ages. I thought that you two were the bad guys. Then the wolves showed up, and I thought, well, which one shall I kill first? It was only when I saw that they were turning into monsters that I thought, no way Jose, this is not a fair fight. So, I said, Lisa, let's help them first, and then maybe kill them after. Anyway, why don't you let me come with you? I am a very good fighter, you know?"

"No thank you," replied Kormo. "I think that you shall make your way back home."

"Home! No way Jose, my life in the Blue Kingdom was boring. Anyway, in that case, I have nothing else to do here. See you later alligators." As she said that her body disappeared against a tree. Then, when everyone thought she was gone, she showed up again. "Hey, now you see me, now you don't!"

"Lisa, go away!" shouted Angel. "Alright, I am leaving, but if you change your mind, I will be around."

Chapter 10
The reunion

The next morning at the Temple of Tarragon everyone was happy and uplifted. "Kormo!" shouted one of the female animen that lived at the temple.
"Yes, how can I help you?"
"Your father wants to see you."
"All right, I am on my way."
As he walked into the room Evenko was sitting in bed.
"Father, do you want to see me?"
"Yes, son, the members of the chamber are here. Find Angel and make your way to the main salon." At that moment Evenko wanted to stand up but he was too weak to do it on his own, so Kormo tried to help him.
"Father, let me take you to the salon. I shall find Angel after." "No, son, you must go now. There are plenty of people here to help me out."
"Alright, father, as you wish."

Later, Angel and Kormo arrived at the other part of the temple. Around a huge round table, Evenko introduced them to Mono, the leader of the apes. Mono was very muscular with a strong look of determination on his face. His chest was big, and he looked ready for battle.
"I just met him yesterday," said Angel, as he acknowledged him from the gorilla kingdom.
Next to Mono was Rayon, the leader of the deer. "Sorry for what happened to your people," said Angel.
"No worries," Rayon replied. "We are glad that you are here, our misery is about to come to an end."

Next was Toro, the leader of the buffalos. "Toro, it's a pleasure meeting you. It will be an honour to go to battle next to you." Next to Toro was Kormo.

"Gentleman, I thank you all for coming here today as we all know my father is not well, but we shall do this in his name and the name of everyone that we have lost. Please allow me to introduce to you the new member of the chamber of peace, Kea the eagle girl."

"Kea, I thought I'd never see you again, my friend," said Angel. "So, you knew the location of the temple all this time?"

"Yes, I did, but you needed to find it by yourself, to be honest. I am glad that you made it."

"Hey guys, do you know each other?" asked Kormo.

"Yes, she saved my life," said Angel.

"Impressive," said Evenko. "Kea, thank you for accepting my invitation to join the chamber and for saving my son's life."

Seconds later Evenko turned his attention toward the others. "Ladies and gentlemen, may I have your attention please? I am so happy to announce that my beloved son has been chosen to carry the medallion of Tempo. Today he will share with all of us the secrets of transformation. Are you ready? Son, say what you need to say."

"Gentlemen, my name is Angel. I have travelled through the parallel passages to share with you all the secrets of transformation."

At that point, Angel told them about the Fountain of Life, the chanting to the gods, and everything he remembered. After the revelation, everyone was confident that their people were going to be able to fully transform. During the meeting the members of the chamber discussed when and how they were going to face their enemies' ones and for all. After a few hours of discussion, everyone returned to their villages to prepare for war.

The next day, Kea and Kormo went back to the orphanage, because it was one of those days when the two of them helped with whatever they could. Later that night, the two of them decided to sleep at the orphanage, just like they had done so many times before.

Meanwhile, at the wolf stronghold, Marmaton had gathered his creatures together. "Creatures of the night, in the last couple of days, we have lost some of our gifted hunters. They were great brothers, good fathers, and loyal pack members. It is time to make the animen species pay for what they have done."

As he finished his sentence the rest of the creatures started shouting, "No mercy, no mercy!"

"Tonight, we are going to burn down the Orphanage of Tarragon with everyone inside," Marmaton said.

Meanwhile, at the orphanage, Kormo was sat outside taking in some fresh air. Just when he was about to walk back inside, he heard a noise coming from the dark. It was not a significant noise, but for the blind boy any noise could mean something, so he walked toward the edge of the long corridor then placed his hand on the corner post. Immediately he saw hundreds of torches approaching the direction of the orphanage. Kormo quickly returned inside. "Kea, wake up."

"What is going on, Kormo?"

"The wolves are coming; we must evacuate the orphanage now."

Kea sounded the huge bell that hung on a particular part of the orphanage. Suddenly, there was panic among the young children and the helpers trying to get everyone inside the underground tunnel that led to a safe place far from the danger. Moments later, Marmaton's very own children, the

Fetus, had reach the location followed by a massive pack of wolves and bats. The Fetus were two teenage brothers from Marmaton and Tina, the bat's former leader. They were twins but looked different: one was a bat and the other was a wolf.

Both had a condition that made them big in size but small in their brain. For that reason, all they knew was how to cause pain to others and were responsible for many atrocities across the kingdom.

The two brothers had grown separated from one another, locked up in a special cage inside the cave because every time they got together, they were like a lethal weapon. As they reached the orphanage one of the brothers shouted, "Attack!" Then, in a matter of minutes, the wolves were setting fire to the orphanage, while the others started to shoot arrows. At the same time the bats were flying above, dropping torches on the roof and through the windows, while othjers were ambushing anyone who tried to escape.

Chapter 11
The revelation

Meanwhile, somewhere inside the Temple of Tarragon, Sarchus felt that his best friend was in trouble. Somehow, he managed to set himself free from his chain and rushed to help him. As soon as Sarchus arrived, the fetus wolf was about to make a killer attack on Kormo. Furious and ready to die for his friend, Sarchus launched into the fetus, forcing him to roll down the hill near to the river. As the two creatures attacked each other with ferocity, Sarchus fell into the water. He struggled to stay safe, dragging the wolf with him. Suddenly the rushing waters took both far down the river.

At that moment the boy was worried about his friend, but there was no time to lose. He turned back in the direction from where he could hear the struggle between Kea and the rest of the warriors against the fetus bat and his companions. As he approached the spot where the fighting was taking place, the fetus bat launched himself at him. Kormo struggled to set himself free from the creature, but the bat was powerful and in a matter of seconds he took off, taking with him our beloved Kormo. At that moment, just as he was about to get away, Kea shot an arrow one more time and managed to hit accurately, but the creature did not fall. Instead, he kept flying into the darkness as his body started to turn into stone.

Kea then flew after them, but the creature was not anywhere to be seen. Back at the burning orphanage, many animen were killed trying to protect their people. Some wolves were still fighting as animals, while the others were transformed into monsters. When the battle was over, the surviving animen arrived at the Temple of Tarragon. Sadly, for all of them, the night had more surprises in store. On arrival, Kea noticed that everything was silent. When she asked what happened, she found out that Evenko, the leader, had fallen very ill.

Inside the room, Evenko was giving Angel his final words. "Angel, I am sad to tell you that my time is almost over, but before I go, there is something important that you must know. Son, Faith, and I are not your biological parents. Fifteen years ago, a day before the wolves first appeared, a terrible storm fell on Tempo. Rain and thunders came down from the sky causing panic among the animen. That day in the middle of the confusion I found you in the bushes. Your clothing indicated that you were not from around here. On your right arm, there was a bracelet with the name Angel. Next to you we found a tiny little ferret. For some reason, he did not want to give up on you. It looked like he was trying to protect you. It was then when I took you home to Faith, my wife, that she immediately fell in love with you."

"Then, when the magical bridge of Vida opened, Faith took you with her to the invisible island. For many years I thought I would never see you again, but here you are. Time brought you back to me, Angel. It is important to know that time is an expensive commodity. It is the only thing that we spend but can never get back. Unfortunately, we never know how much time we have left until it runs out. I would have loved to experience the power of transformation at least one in my lifetime, but look at me, my time is over." As Evenko said his last words his body started to deteriorate. He transformed into small flowers that spread across the room, illuminating everything before drifting out of the small window.

At that point, Angel could not hold it for any longer. "Don't do this to me... Dad, please come back." Suddenly, he stormed out of the room straight into the darkness.

Minutes later, Kea entered the room, but there was no sign of Angel. Immediately she went after him. "Have you seen Angel?"

"He walked in that direction," replied a female animen. Kea knew how dangerous the night could be for anyone to be wandering along on the forest, especially after what happened earlier at the orphanage.

"Guys, get as many animen as possible. Send for help if you have to, but find Angel, please."

"What about you, where are you going?"

"I am going to find Kormo." Minutes later, she also took to the other side of the forest with a small group of animen to search for Kormo, hoping that he would still be alive.

Chapter 12
The White Wolf

After storming out of the Temple of Tarragon following the passing of Evenko, Angel sat down on a rock, crying from a mix of sadness and confusion. Then, he started to hear the voice of his mother. "Angel let's go home, there is nothing else to do here. Come to me, my son." Suddenly, a female figure arrived in the distance.

"Mum, is that you?" At that point, Angel stood up and started to walk in the direction of the female. "Mum, why are you walking away from me?" Minutes into his walk, Angel acknowledged that the image of his mother was just a hallucination caused by recent events, but at that point, he had already gone too far deep into the unknown. As he turned around trying to find his way back to the temple, a group of wolves appeared. Their pointy ears, and their bare teeth indicated that the creatures were ready to kill. Understanding that he had been ambushed by the rather aggressive creatures and with no strength to fight or produce any magic, Angel decided to run. Then, after a rather long chase through the forest, he fell into a trap.

Soon after, as the wolves carried him around the path with his hands and feet tied up, the chant of Vida came into his head. Hi lala, hi lala, ole ole mo, hi lala, hi lala, ole ole mo! Gods of Tempo, gods of Tempo thank you for the power of transformation. As the chant became more and more prominent, a strange sensation of transformation took over Angel's body. What is happening? he thought. I thought that I was already over the transformation process. Then, without warning, his feet started to rip apart as if a different creature was coming out of him. His arms became stronger and were forming some sort of animal look. It was then when he knew that he was transforming into something big. Suddenly, his body was becoming hairy. He could feel his head getting bigger and taking on an unusual shape.

Then, a long skull began forming above his brain. His mouth was changing, large jaw muscles began forming inside of it, and massive teeth started to overtake his natural teeth. At that point, the sound of the dry grass under the feet of the wolves was audible, and the look and smell of those who were still walking next to them in their animal form made him feel irritated. Suddenly, the sky started to glow as if a real circle of life was forming right above them. Then, as the trees gave way to the clarity of the night, the chant was more and more clear in his head. Hi lala, hi lala, ole ole mo, hi lala, hi lala, ole ole mo! Gods of Tempo, gods of Tempo thank you for the power of transformation.
At that point, the full moon came out of its resting place to witness what was about to happen.

When the wolves walked into the plain, the full moon reflected on Angel's face. He suddenly let out a powerful howl that resonated in every corner of Tempo as he transformed into a gigantic white wolf.

Moments later, animen from every corner of the kingdom
started to descend in the direction of the Forest of the Dead
ready to battle. It was clear to them that it was the call of
the chosen one. Meanwhile, Marmaton, already angry and
sad about the loss of his beloved children, the fetus, and
some members of the pack, had just heard the news that the
chosen one had transformed into a wolf. Twice as angry, he

walked toward a metal cage, then spoke to a creature on the inside. "My child, it seems to me that the medallion of Tempo has given the boy incredible powers. Under any circumstances, the power of transformation can be passed into the animen species, because, with such power, they will become invincible. For that reason, I command you, my child, to get out there and bring me the medallion of Tempo. If you do that, I shall give you the gift of eternity."

As he finished his words, he opened the door of the cage from where a massive two-headed wolf came out. As the creature stood in front of Marmaton, his body began to transform into a giant monster. Then, when the transformation was complete, the monster stormed into the forest followed by twenty strong wolves.

Meanwhile, on the other end of the forest, the animen of Tempo were approaching the forest of dead carrying torches, also armed with bows and arrows, swords, axes, heavy chains, and so on, while chanting to the gods: "Hilala hi lalal ole ole mo, hi lala hi lala ho le ole mo. Gods of Tempo, gods of Tempo, thank you for the power of transformation." As the animen ran through the forest their bodies began to transform into their animal centres for the first time. The gorillas were also descending from the mountains, the elders storming down the path, while the younger ones were jumping from one tree to another, anxious to get to the battleground. From the other side of the forest, deer, bulls, and rhinos were also approaching the Forest of the Dead, with only one mission on mind: kill or be killed.

Chapter 13
The Rescue

Meanwhile, somewhere not too far away, Kea with a group of animen were still searching for Kormo when they heard the loud howl of the white wolf. Without hesitation, the group returned to Tempo, ready to join the fight. At the same time, right at the edge of Tundra, Kormo had found himself in new territory. First, he struggled to get himself out from under the gigantic fetus bat whose body had turned into stone after being shot by Kea. As soon as he managed to free himself, he tried to locate his staff but could not find it. Then, he heard predators communicating from different parts of that doomed jungle. He had no idea where he was, but somehow the smell, the dry soil, and the different sounds indicated that he was in an unfamiliar place. As he walked in the direction to where he thought he could find his way around, a group of strange creatures approached him. He could feel their dark energy.

The creatures were human and looked like animen but were different from the animen of Tempo. They had human faces with animal teeth. They were wearing long ropes and carrying long axes, their hands and arms were pure bones like skeleton, their ears were big as if adapted to hear the most insignificant noise, and their eyes symbolised the dead.

The boy stood still to comprehend their intentions and locate their position and distance from him. "My name is Kormo. I come in peace. Please reveal yourself." The problem was that the creatures did not seem to have understood him. Instead, they charged into the boy, determined to kill him.

Kormo tried to defend himself using his fighting skills, but the creatures were mean and very competent too. At that point he realised that without his staff there was not much he could do, so he ran for his life, as he approached a plain grassy area, the boy could hear the chasers all around him. He quickly climbed a tree. Suddenly, the creatures started to shake the tree trying to make him fall to the ground.

Moments later he heard them screaming. Soon, he realised that there was an aggressive creature slaughtering them. From his position he could feel the energy, but he could not see what was happening. After a few minutes, there was silence. At that point Kormo did not know if he had been saved, or if he was going to be next. After some consideration he let go of the branch and landed on the ground. As he did so, he felt the presence of somebody walking toward him. He could sense that whatever it was, was very big. This time, panic invaded his blood system. He was almost sure that he was going to die. As the creature got closer and closer to him, he recognised the smell. He stood still for a moment, then he said, "Sarchus, is that you?"

Next, he extended his arms trying to touch the creature. As his hands contacted the animal, he could see his face. At that moment the two of them embraced with a hug. Sarchus then grabbed Kormo's staff using his mouth and gently placed it into his hands.

"You have found my staff, good boy!" Sarchus kneeled in front of him, and immediately Kormo climbed into his back. "Come on, boy, let's go home."

Meanwhile on Tempo, just as it was fifteen years earlier, animen, wolves, and bats were fighting for survival. There was a lot of fire, noise, and confusion all over the place. The forest had become a battleground.

"This way!" said the deer, as he guided his people through the forest.

"What is happening?" shouted Kea as she caught up with them. "Can't you see? The battle has begun," replied one of the massive deer as he kept running down toward the action.

"Where is Angel?" Kea asked.

"There he is," replied another deer as he pointed to the white wolf."

"Oh my! Angel, is that you?" At that point, the massive white wolf was covered in blood and bruises.

"You didn't think you would do it without me, did you?"

Suddenly the massive two-headed wolf appeared, causing panic among the rest of the animen, including his kind.

The vicious creature soon located the white wolf, and straight away attacked him. As the creatures made contact, Kea came to help, but could not find a clear shot. She knew that she needed to wait for the right moment to shoot.

At the same time, the animen kept chanting to the gods of Tempo. "Hilala hi lalala ole ole mo, hi lala, hi lalla, ole ole mo." As the chant continued some of the eagles began transforming in mid-air into massive birds, while others, including Kea, remained in their usual animen form. Immediately, the birds started to hunt down bats and wolves picking them up with their strong talons. As they did, they would fly as high as they could before letting their prey fall to the ground. At the same time, the two-headed wolf started to show signs of weakness. It was a matter of time before he went down. In the middle of the struggle, the beast took down a few unlucky animen that were fighting too close to him.

Chapter 14
The Hands of God

As the fight continued, the white wolf fell on the ground exhausted. A moment later, the two-headed wolf moved closer to him, then raised an axe ready to finish him off. Luckily, Kea found the perfect opportunity to shoot an arrow at him, and it hit right on target. The beast made a terrifying howl. It was a mix of anger and pain, on that instant part of his body started to turn into stone, but he kept moving forward, killing anything in his path. After a couple of shots from Kea, the massive creature was finally taken down.

Shortly after, Marmaton, the alpha himself, showed up. His face was covered with a scar, and he had only one eye. His expression was vicious, his ears erect, and his mouth showed his deadly teeth. His skin was hard, and his long tail indicated danger. At that point, hundreds of wolves stood next to him, carrying all sort of weapons. Some had already transformed, while others were still in their animal form. At the same time, the white wolves were also surrounded by hundreds of animen. There were a lot of rhinos, buffaloes, deer, gorillas, and eagles. As the two groups faced each other on the open plain, the white wolf ordered his animen to drop their weapon. At that point, the wolves could not believe what they were seeing.

For a moment some of the wolves wanted to attack, then the animen started shouting, "Drop, drop, drop!" The sound became louder and louder. Marmaton ordered his creatures to drop their weapons. It was the first time that the animen, wolves, and bats were about to face each other without weapons, but before that happened, the two leaders needed to battle one on one.

At that point, the white wolf stepped forward, ready to fight. "Good luck, my friend," said Kea, as she and the others stepped back to allow him more room. Then, Marmaton stepped forward.

As the two of them ran toward each other, the sky turned purple, then thunder and lightning started to strike. For a short time, there was total silence, then the two leaders clashed.

In the middle of the struggle, Marmaton yowled a couple of terrifying howls, attracting the attention of more wolves and bats. As the fight intensified, the white wolf ended up on the ground. He was bleeding and unable to continue the fights. At that moment, from out of nowhere, Ferret appeared. 'Angel, stand up. You are the chosen one, the animen kind need you now more than ever." Suddenly, the white wolf started to feel stronger, and he knew that he had another chance. He was prepared to take it.

In the meantime, from the other side of the forest, a huge animal was approaching at a high speed. As the creature got out into the open, Kea noticed that it was Sarchus, the young predator that she rescued from Tundra, the forbidden island. On his back was Kormo, the blind boy. At that point, she was so happy to see her two friends alive and well.

At soon as Sarchus entered the open, the chant of Vida intensified, at that moment Kormo jumped of his back, then, before she could say anything the boy let go a massive roar as he transformed into a black panther.

His body was big and strong, and his expression was very scary. Soon, he had hold of a wolf and in a matter of seconds killed him. Then, the blind panther followed a bat up a tree. As the bat intended to fly off, he jumped, catching the creature in mid-air. By the time their bodies reached the ground the bat was already dead. At that moment there was panic among some of the wolves as the angry blind panther launched itself toward more creatures.

However, as more wolves and bats kept showing up, Ferret, who was still around, started to panic. "Oh my, I must do something. I must do something!" He kneeled to the ground, then, looking up to the sky, said, "We need more helping hands now." At that point everything paused and there was total silence for a short time. Surprisingly the ground started shaking, then large magical hands began to emerge from down under. The hands then started to grab wolves and bats, taking them back deep into the ground. However, as more wolves and bats kept showing up, Ferret, who was still around, started to panic. "Oh my, I must do something. I must do something!" He kneeled to the ground, then, looking up to the sky, said, "We need more helping hands now." At that point everything paused and there was total silence for a short time. Surprisingly the ground started shaking, then large magical hands began to emerge from down under. The hands then started to grab wolves and bats, taking them back deep into the ground.

Meanwhile, the white wolf was still struggling against Marmaton, when suddenly Sarchus manage to grab his head with his huge mouth, producing a killer bite. At that point, the alpha let out a very loud cry of pain, then fell to the ground. For an instant he looked dead, but no one was sure. At that moment, the rest of the wolves started making some very aggressive howls. Moments later, every single wolf turned their attention oward Sarchus. "Attack!" shouted one of the wolves. Soon,

a few wolves were trying to take down Sarchus. Then, the
blind panther heard his friend struggling, so he launched
himself forward trying to defend him.

At that moment, from the distance, the white wolf who had just acknowledged the danger shouted, "Kormo no, it is too dangerous!" However, the blind panther did not seem to have heard him, so he shouted again, "Kormo no, it is too dangerous!"

Then, from out of nowhere, Marmaton stood up holding a broken sword, ready to strike. Luckily, Dangerous, the young offspring that they previously saved from the fire, appeared. He grabbed Marmaton and dragged him away as he finished him off. Suddenly, the rest of the wolves began to get a hold of their weapon, and so did the animen of Tempo. At that point, once again hundreds of animen ran toward the massive army of wolves while shooting arrows a them. For a good period, they clashed with all their powers, but the wolves started to become weaker and weaker as the fight went on. Not long after, the moon gave way to the daylight as a sign that Tempo's darkest hours had come to ar end. Suddenly, the surviving wolves knew that without Marmaton there was no point in carrying on the fight, so they began to transform back into animals as they ran off across the river away from Tempo.

When the battle was finally over, the animen began to transform back into their usual human-like forms. Then, as they celebrated victory, the bodies of those who died in battle transformed into thousands of small lighting flowers, then took to the sky, while the corps of the wolves and bats turned to ashes right at the spot, except for the ones shot by Kea, who remained as massive sculpture-like stones.

Chapter 15
The New World

It was early morning in Tempo. That day, happiness had taken over every single animen. Suddenly, the magical bridge that separated Tempo with Vida appeared. Immediately, the animen ran toward the bridge to welcome their loved ones with open arms. Angel was looking forward to seeing his beloved mum. Then, he spotted her among the crowd. As they got together, the two of them embraced in a long-deserved hug without words. Then, Angel broke the silence.

"He did not make it, Mum. I tried, but he did not get to experience the transformation."

"Don't be sad, my boy, for some reason I had a strange sensation that he came to say goodbye to me. I am glad that you got to meet him, but there is something you must know." "Mum, I know everything, he has already told me." "I am sorry, son, I am sure you will get to know who your real parents are. Forgive me for not telling you earlier, but there is another thing that you must know."

"What is it, Mum?"

"Angel, it is time for me to return home, my time here is over. Only the young animen like you will be able to experience the transformation for years to come."

"But, Mum, I need you here with us, everything will be different now that the wolves are gone."

"Son, there is nothing I can do, the gods have already chosen me as well as many others, look around us."

From the distance Angel could see how other elders were disintegrating into hundreds of lighting flowers just like his father and all the others had done. Everyone was sad to see what was happening. In a matter of minutes all the elders were gone. All he had was a handful of tiny flowers from his mother's hands.

"Angel, I know that you must be very sad," said Kea as she approached him. "Just remember this is the circle of life, our elders will always have to go to that place called home. For sure we will meet them again when our time runs out. At least we could see a new beginning."

After hearing Kea's words, Angel felt a lot better. Then, he used the occasion to stand on a rock ready to speak to his people. "Animen of Tempo, my name is Angel. I am here to tell you that from this day on, you can be whatever you want to be, do what you like to do, go wherever you wish to go. You no longer must live a life that you don't want to live. Animen of Tempo are you ready to transform one more time?"

"Yeah!" screamed the excited crowd. At that very moment, the trees started changing. Everything was becoming green and beautiful again. It was amazing to see how the animen transformed into different animals. Moments later, as everyone enjoyed the transformation, the sky started to turn dark. There were strong winds and dry thunder, and then suddenly a god-like face formed high up in the clouds. Everything stood still.

"Angel, today you have earned your place among the animen species. For that reason, we name you the guardian of the Seven Kingdoms of Tempo. Now, you must help them to fulfil their destiny before their time runs out," the face said.

Angel did not know what to think. There were a lot of questions rushing through his head. Then, as the face vanished, Angel looked at the sky and shouted "Hey, why me?" Suddenly, another face formed up on the cloud. This time it was a female.

"Angel, I am very proud of you. By claiming your place alongside the animen species, you have also reclaimed your place in Tempo among the gods and the celestial angels. Your destiny has been written, but the animen species are still in danger. You must travel to the Triangle of Spectra before it is too late."

"Who are you?" shouted Angel.

"I am Vida, your mother." After the final word, the face vanished.

At that very moment, Ferret was passing by. "Ferret, come here now!" shouted Angel. "It is time for you to tell me everything you know about me."

"Angel, sixteen years ago, Vida, the angel of life, had a romantic relationship with one of the gods' greatest enemies. When he found out your mum was expecting a baby, he became very upset, then after you were born, he tries to kill you on many occasions. Luckily, Hora, the angel of time, persuaded her sister to send you into the animen kingdom, because it was the only place where your father could never find you."

There was a sad expression on Angel's face. "Are you saying that I am an angel?"

"Yes, my boy, Angel is a real angel, a very special one."

"Ferret, I had spent all my life thinking that I was an animen, how could it be? You just saw me out there transformed into a wolf. How that could be even possible?"

"Angel, if you are alive, anything is possible. What happened there was that you accessed the powers of transformation. Any living creature has access to it, the problem is that not many make use of it."

"All right, I understand, but what happened to my wings, how could I be an angel without wings?"

"Ah, the wings, well, to send Angel to the animen kingdom, angel's wings needed to be taken away. However, Angel's mother created a special place on the celestial palace where she kept hold of them, because that was the only way Angel could have survived down here. Also, by keeping Angel's wings, she could track Angel's development. As Angel grew older, his wings grew bigger. When Angel was ill, the wings got ill. If Angel was happy his wings flapped and shined with happiness too. Angel's mum had always loved her little angel, which is why she sent Ferret into the Seven Kingdoms of Tempo, to be by Angel's side. Ferret's mission was to always protect Angel, until the time was right for Angel to go back to where he belongs."

As the conversation came to an end, a magic circle started forming around them. "What is happening?" asked Angel, as the circle started to grow bigger. "I am not ready to go, what about my friends?"

"Don't panic, young Angel, it is destiny unfolding at this very moment. The time has come, just trust the process," said Ferret. Suddenly the circle of life started to rotate faster and faster, dragging then inside of the portal as it transported them through the passages of the universe into the unknown.

At the same time Kea and Kormo approached from the other side. Next to them was a huge young animen. His body was strong and hairy, but his facial expressions indicated he was a bit confused, his name was Sarchus.

End of

The Chronicles of Tempo

Part One

Angel

Kormo

Angel

Kormo

Kea

Lisa

Sarchus

Sarchus

Marmaton

Two Head Twins

Fetus Bat

Fetus Wolf

The Wolves Pack

The Skeleton Man

Animen Kingdom Books

Printed in Great Britain
by Amazon

23423873R00051